Vampire School

Teacher

Screecher

For Theo and Tara
P.B.
For my Mum
C.H.

First published in Great Britain in 2011
by Boxer Books Limited.

www.boxerbooks.com

Based on an original idea by Chris Harrison
Text copyright © 2011 Peter Bently
Illustrations copyright © 2011 Chris Harrison

The illustrations were prepared using biro and watercolour paints
The text is set in Blackmoor Plain and Adobe Caslon

ISBN 978-1-907967-02-3

1 3 5 7 9 10 8 6 4 2

Printed in Great Britain

Vampire School

Teacher Screecher

Written by Peter Bently

Illustrated by Chris Harrison

Boxer Books

Contents

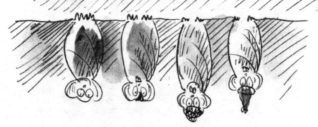

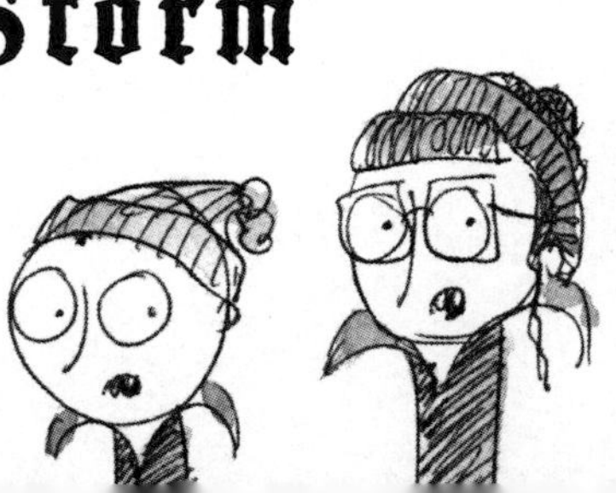

Chapter 1
Bat Flu

One evening, Lee Price's mum walked into his bedroom and stopped. The bedroom looked empty.

"Hurry up, you three – wherever you are," said Mrs Price. "It's twenty to nine.

You'll be late for school!"
"We're in here," said Lee's
voice from the wardrobe.
"We've all turned into bats.
Hang on."
Lee fluttered out of the
wardrobe followed by his best
friends,

Bella Williams and Billy
Pratt.

"We were doing some skulking
practice," said Lee.

Lee, Bella and Billy went to
St Orlok's Primary School for
young vampires. Their teacher,
Miss Gargoyle, taught them
important vampire skills, like
how to change into bats and
the Three S's – Swooping,
Swerving and Skulking.

"Right," said Mrs Price. "Now
off to school. Dad's asleep
in bed with bat flu so it'll be

quieter if you leave through
the window."

Mrs Price opened the bedroom
window and Lee, Billy and
Bella flew out into the night.
Ten minutes later they flapped
through the school gates and
changed back into vampire form.

A strange black van was parked nearby. On the side of the van it said:

Frances & Kenneth Styne & Company

The driver was helping Mr Eric Gore, the school's zombie caretaker, to lug an enormous crate out of the van. The crate was nearly three metres long.

"Frances and Kenneth Styne,"
said Lee. "I think that's a shop
in town. I wonder what's in
the crate?"
Mr Gore looked at
them gloomily.
"Vouldn't you like
to know,
eh?" he
droned.
"Nosy
little vampire brats!"
"Er – good morning, Mr
Gore," said Lee as politely as
he could.

"Ye-e-e-s!" groaned Mr Gore, patting the crate. "Oh yes. A very good mornink indeed!"

He opened his mouth and
made a weird noise like
someone coughing, gargling
and throwing up all at the
same time.

"Hrurgh! Hrurgh! Hrurgh!"

"Good grief," whispered
Lee. "Old Gore's actually
laughing!"

"Wow!" said
Billy. "Do you
think he's sick?
There's a lot of
bat flu about."

"Don't be silly," said Bella.
"Only vampires get bat flu.
And bats, of course."
"So why is he so cheerful?"
said Billy. "Old Gore doesn't
do cheerful."
"I bet it's something to do
with that crate," said Lee.

"Maybe it's a new floor polisher. He's always moaning about the old one."
Lee was right. It was something to do with the crate. But it wasn't a new floor polisher. Inside the crate was something much, much worse.

Chapter 2
Miss Fitt

Lee, Bella and Billy entered their classroom to see Mrs Garlick, the school head teacher.

"Settle down, please, Miss Gargoyle's class!" said Mrs Garlick. "I am afraid Miss Gargoyle has a nasty case of bat flu. She will be off school for at least two weeks."

"Oh, poor Miss Gargoyle!" said Bella.

"While Miss Gargoyle is away you will have a supply teacher," said Mrs Garlick. "She has also worked at Chaney Street First School and Mr Savage, the head teacher, tells me that she is very nice." Chaney Street was the werewolf primary school down the road. "In fact she should be here any min—"

She was interrupted by a noise in the corridor.

STOMP!
STOMP!
STOMP!
STOMP!

"Yikes!" said Lee, as the whole classroom shook. "What on earth is that?"

STOMP!
STOMP!
STOMP!

The heavy stomping sound
was getting louder and louder.
And closer and closer.

STOMP!
STOMP!
STOMP!

Tables wobbled and windows
rattled. Pencils and crayons
jumped out of pots.

Mrs Garlick's glasses fell off her nose. The Monster Munches that Big Herb was secretly scoffing bounced out of the packet and onto the floor.

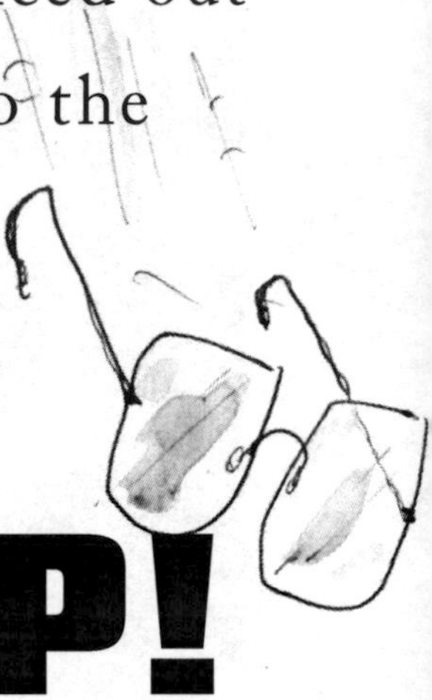

STOMP!

STOMP!

STOMP!

The noise stopped. Everyone held their breath. Then–

CRUNCH!

SPLINTER!

CRACK!

The classroom door was torn off its hinges. It toppled to the ground with a

KER-RASH!

But the young vampires weren't looking at the door.

They were looking at what was standing in the doorway.

It was three metres tall and two metres wide. It was dressed completely in black and clutched a little pink handbag. Two stiff plaits stuck out horizontally from its head. And two steel bolts stuck out horizontally from its neck.

Attached to one of the bolts
was a label that said:

PROPERTY OF

F. AND K. STYNE & CO.

It was a monster.

The children gasped.

"Now we know what was in
that crate!" whispered Lee.

"SILENCE!"

roared the monster.

Mrs Garlick smiled
nervously.

"Ah, children," she said.
"Erm – allow me to introduce
Miss Fitt. Your new teacher."

Chapter 3
Number Nightmare

As Mrs Garlick slipped hastily out of the room, Miss Fitt lurched to the front of the classroom like a walking earthquake. She turned and slowly stared around the class.

"SILENCE!"

she bellowed, even though it was so quiet you could hear a pin drop. "There will be no noise in my class! Now get out your maths books!"

A flutter of grumbles went around the room.

"SILENCE!"

hollered Miss Fitt.

Bella put her hand up.

"Please, Miss," she said. "We have vampire history now, not maths. We don't have maths till after break."

"SILENCE!"

screeched Miss Fitt. "If I say we have maths, we have maths! What is your name, girl?"

"B-Bella Williams, Miss."

"What is thirty-seven times thirty-seven? You have five seconds!" demanded Miss Fitt.

Bella was really good at maths and was about to give the answer when Miss Fitt snapped, "Time's up! Hah! As I thought! Vampires know nothing! You will all stay in during break and write out

your thirty-seven times table
thirty-seven times!"

"Aw, Miss!" groaned the
class.

"SILENCE!"

roared Miss Fitt. "Never
speak with your mouth open!
Vampires should be seen and
not heard! And preferably not
seen either!"

Lee, Bella and Billy swapped glances.

"No wonder old Gore was so happy!" whispered Lee.

"SILENCE!

Vampires are a lazy bunch of ghoul-for-nothings! Lying around in coffins all day when they could be doing MATHS!"

Grabbing a red marker pen, Miss Fitt stomped up to the big timetable on the classroom wall.

"I'm not teaching any of this useless vampire nonsense.

Vampire history indeed!"

She drew a thick line through vampire history and wrote MATHS instead.

"And what's this? Bat lessons?" spat Miss Fitt.

"Ridiculous! If vampires were meant to fly they would have wings already, without any of this changing into bats rubbish!"

So out went bat lessons, and in went – more MATHS.

By the time Miss Fitt had finished, the timetable looked like this:

	9.00–9.45pm	9.45–10.30pm	10.30–10.50pm	10.50pm–12.15am	12.15–1.15am	1.15–2.15am	2.15–3.15am
day	MATHS Bat lessons	MATHS Transylvanian made easy	B	MATHS English	L	MATHS Scary staring	GOOD! Maths
day	MATHS Vampire history	MATHS English	R	Very good! Maths	U	MATHS Vampire science	MATHS PE (Prowling exercises)
nesday	MATHS English	MATHS Menacing music	E	MATHS Vampire self defence	N	MATHS Cooking without garlic	MATHS Mastering mirrors
hursday	MATHS Quite right too!	MATHS Vampire geography	A	MATHS Coffin care	C	MATHS Alarming art	MATHS PE (Prowling exercises)
Friday	School assembly	MATHS English	K	MATHS So it should be!	H	MATHS Transylvanian made easy	MATHS Creepy costumes

Chapter 4
Monster Mystery

"I don't understand," said
Billy. "Mrs Garlick said Miss
Fitt would be nice."

"That's only what the head
of Chaney Street told her,"
said Lee.

"But why would he say it
if it wasn't true?" said Bella.
"Mrs Garlick could have easily
found someone else."

"I know," said Lee. "Let's ask Ollie after school." Ollie Talbot was Lee's werewolf friend at Chaney Street.

"Good idea," agreed Bella.

"He always walks home past the school gate. If we leave dead on time we can catch him."

Unfortunately Bella spoke too soon. During the very last

lesson of the night – maths
instead of PE (prowling
exercises) – Billy accidentally
squashed Bella's toe with his
chair leg.

"Ouch!" cried Bella.
"Careful, Billy!"

"SILENCE!"

screeched Miss Fitt. "So. Bella
Williams. You again, eh? I
might have known!"

"But Miss—" Bella tried to explain.

"SILENCE!"

"It wasn't her fault, Miss," said Billy.

"SILENCE!"

cried Miss Fitt. "I can see you're a pair of regular troublemakers. You will both stay after school and write out 'The square of the hypotenuse is equal to the sum of the squares of the other two sides' two hundred times!

Mrs Garlick will inform your parents of your misbehaviour!"

Bella and Billy looked aghast.

"But, Miss, it was an accident!" cried Lee.

"SILENCE!"

shrieked Miss Fitt. "As you're so keen on your delinquent friends, you can join them in detention!"

Lee, Billy and Bella came out of detention an hour after school had ended.

"Bother," said Bella. "It's starting to rain."

"And we missed Ollie," grumbled Lee.

"No we didn't," cried Billy suddenly. "There he is!"

Ollie was just walking past the school. It wasn't a full moon that night so he looked just like an ordinary boy, apart from his hairy hands.

"Of course," said Lee.
"I forgot he has casketball
practice tonight." Casketball
was a game a bit like
basketball.

"Hey, Ollie!" called Lee.
Ollie came over.

"Hi, Lee!" he said. "Hi, Billy
and Bella! What are you doing
at school so late?"

"Detention," explained Bella. "Miss Gargoyle's off with bat flu. Until she comes back we've got a horrible new teacher."

"We were going to ask you about her," said Lee. "Her name's Miss Fitt."

"What?" said Ollie. "Miss Fitt gave you detention? As in Miss Fitt of Styne and Company?"

"That's her," said Lee.

"Wow!" said Ollie, amazed. "We had Miss Fitt for a month when our teacher broke his hind leg. She was brilliant. She gave us loads of sweets and never got cross!"

This time it was Lee, Bella and Billy who gasped in amazement.

"But do you know the best thing about her?" Ollie went on. "We did hardly any maths.

She said it was boring! How cool is that?" He glanced at his watch. "Yikes! I'll be late for tea. See you!"

As Ollie hurried off, the three vampires just stood there and gawped. Suddenly the main school doors opened and out popped the gloomy, greenish face of Mr Gore.

He looked at the sky and stuck a grubby hand into the rain, which was falling more heavily now.

"It is startink!" he muttered to himself. "Good! Hrurgh!

Hrurgh!" Then he spotted Lee, Bella and Billy. "Hey! Vot are you doing, you nosy vampire kids? School is closed! Clear off!"

Mr Gore slammed the door and the three vampires heard the loud sliding of bolts and the rattling of keys in the lock.

"Come on," said Lee. "I've had enough of school for one night."

"Me too," said Bella.

With a POP! POP! POP! they all turned into bats.

They were about to head for home when they heard a horribly familiar noise. It was coming from somewhere behind the school doors:

STOMP! STOMP! STOMP! STOMP!

"Yikes, it's her!" squeaked Billy. "I'm off!"

"Hang on," said Lee. "Didn't old Gore just lock up?"

"Yes," said Billy. "Why?"

"Think about it," said Lee. "If the school is locked for the night, why is Miss Fitt still in the building?"

Chapter 5
The Attic

Lee, Billy and Bella flew up to the school doors and listened.

"It sounds like she's going upstairs," said Lee. "Come on!"

They reached the first floor

windows just as Miss Fitt lumbered onto the landing. But she didn't stop there. Trailed by the three vampire bats, she climbed the stairs all the way to the top floor. There were no classrooms on this floor, only storerooms. It was a part of St Orlok's the young vampires had never been to.

"Now what?" said Lee, as they skulked under the gutter out of sight. "There's nowhere else for her to go."

"Not quite," said Billy. "Look!"

Slowly, Miss Fitt crossed the landing. In one dark and dingy corner was a grimy door. She grabbed the handle and turned it. As the door opened Lee, Bella and Billy could clearly read the words on it:

MR E. GORE
CARETAKER
VAMPIRES KEEP OUT!

"So that's where old Gore hangs out!" exclaimed Lee. "The attic!"

"But why is she going up there?" cried Bella.

Bella almost had to shout to be heard above the rain. There was a rumble of thunder and a gust of wind, and then a voice behind them suddenly said –

"BOO!"

The vampire bats shrieked and nearly jumped out of their fur. They turned to see Lee's friend Boris, a real bat who lived in the school clock tower.

"Boris!" yelled Lee. "Don't do that!"

"Sorry!" chuckled Boris. "I didn't realise vampires were scared of bats! Tee-hee!"

As he spoke, Miss Fitt lurched through the attic door and slammed it behind her. They heard her stomping up the stairs.

"Hey," said Boris. "Who was that monster?"

"It's Miss Fitt," said Billy. "She's our teacher while Miss Gargoyle is ill."

"Bad luck!"
said Boris. "What's she doing
in old Gore's attic?"

"We'd love to find out," said
Lee.

"No problemo!" said Boris.
"We can use the hole."

"Hole? What hole?" asked Lee.

"I'll show you," said Boris.
"Come on!"

Lee, Bella and Billy followed Boris out into the driving rain and howling wind. They landed on the roof by a gap where a tile was missing.

"That's weird," said Lee. "I've never noticed that hole before."

"It wasn't there until today," said Boris. "Old Gore took the tile out at lunchtime. I saw him do it."

"Why would he do that?" said Lee.

The wind suddenly died down and the four bats heard voices below.

"Ah, Miss Fitt, Miss Fitt! Velcome, velcome!" groaned Gore. "You are looking most elegant zis eefnink!"

"SILENCE, fool!" groaned Miss Fitt. "Hurry! Can't go on... much longer... Almost... run... out."

"Do not worry, Miss Fitt, do not worry! Everysink is almost ready! Come over here and I'll just..."

FLASH! BOOM!

A great thunderclap made all the bats jump and drowned out the rest of Mr Gore's words.

"What does he mean?" cried Lee as the wind picked up again. "What has Miss Fitt almost run out of? And what is almost ready?"

"Why don't we take a look?" said Boris.

"No way!" said Billy. "Old

Gore's bound
to see us!"
There was
another flash of
lightning, and this
time the thunder was so
loud that the tiles rattled.
"Let's get inside," said Lee.
"It's better than being out in
this storm!"

He peeped over the edge of the hole. "All clear," he said. "Come on!"

One by one they slipped through the hole – and down into old Gore's attic.

Chapter 6
The Monster Mega Charger

The four bats dangled in the
rafters just under the hole.
Gore had his back to them.
He appeared to be strapping
Miss Fitt to a long black
bench surrounded by electrical
wires and tubes. These all led
to a gigantic machine covered
with knobs and switches and

dials and lights. A flash of
lightning revealed the words
on the machine:

MONSTER MEGA
CHARGER
PROPERTY OF
F. AND K. STYNE & CO.

"Wow," said Boris. "What on
earth is that?"

"Well, it isn't a floor
polisher, that's for certain,"
said Lee.

"I don't like the look of it,"
said Bella.

"I think it's a charging
machine," said Billy. "I read

about them in Junior Science Freakly. They're for recharging monsters when their power runs out. A bit like a battery charger."

"That's it!" said Bella. "When Miss Fitt said she was 'nearly running out', she meant she was nearly running out of power. Old Gore's going to recharge her!"

"Come on," said Lee. "Let's
go closer while his back is turned."

The bats zipped across the
attic to the cobwebby shadows
just above the machine. And
not a moment too soon.

FLASh!

flickered the lightning.

BOOM!

crashed the thunder.

Mr Gore swung round and stared through the hole in the roof.

"Almost time! Almost time!" he whined. "The weather is perfect!"

"S...I...L...E...N...C...E," croaked Miss Fitt, her voice trailing away. "Hurry up, fool!" she rasped.

"Not long now, oh Monstrous One!" droned Gore. "When ze lightning is directly overhead, I will give you a super-duper double-dose of electricity! After zat it will be no more

Miss Nice Monster! Hrurgh!
Hrurgh! Hrurgh!"

Mr Gore clipped a thick
wire to each bolt in Miss Fitt's
neck.

"Yikes," said Lee. "We have
to do something!"

"But what?" said Bella.
"I haven't a clue how that
machine works!"

"Could you work it, Billy?" asked Boris.

"Er... maybe," said Billy. "If we can get close enough without old Gore seeing us."

FLASH! BOOM!

"Almost time! Almost time!" wailed Mr Gore, his eyes wild with joy. "Now for the lightning conductor!"

Mr Gore scuttled across the attic to a shiny metal pole. There was a brass ball at the tip and a heavy stand at the bottom so it wouldn't fall over. Grunting with effort, Gore pushed the pole towards the hole in the roof.

"Quick!" said Lee. "Now's our chance!"

The four bats swooped down to the Monster Mega Charger.

"There should be a special knob here somewhere," said Billy, peering at the buzzing, whirring machine with all its flashing dials and buttons and glowing tubes and different

coloured wires. "Bother! Where is it? It's all very confusing."

FLASH! BOOM!

"Any second now!" grunted Mr Gore. "Hrurgh! Hrurgh!"

The brass tip of the conductor was now sticking out of the hole into the storm.

Gore was attaching a long cable to a socket in the base. The other end of the cable was plugged into the Monster Mega Charger.

Miss Fitt's eyes flicked open.

"Vampires!" she muttered – too quietly for Mr Gore to hear, but loudly enough to startle the bats.

"Ouch!" said Boris, walloping his head on the machine.

"Now!" yelled Gore. "It is time!"

"Oh no!" cried Bella. "Look! We're too late!"

FLA-A A-SH! KERRR-BOOOM!

A stupendous bolt of lightning struck the conductor with a great BANG! As the thunder exploded overhead, brilliant blue sparks flashed down the conductor, along the cable, into the Monster Mega Charger, out through the wires – and into the bolts in Miss Fitt's neck. She jerked and twitched and bounced into the air, nearly snapping her straps.

"Come on!" hissed Lee. "Time we got out of here!"

The bats darted into the rafters just as Gore swung round and lurched back towards the bench.

"It is done! It is done!" wailed Gore, switching off the Monster Mega Charger. "Zose pesky vampires do not know vot is comink! Hrurgh! Hrurgh! Hrurgh!"

As old Gore cackled hysterically, the bats shot out of the attic and into the stormy sky.

"Well, that was a waste of time," said Lee gloomily.

"And now Miss Fitt will be even more horrid," said Bella.

"I'm off home out of the rain," shivered Billy.

"Me too," said Lee.

"And me," said Bella. "See you both at school later—"

She suddenly hesitated.

"Hang on," she gasped. "Where's Boris?"

Chapter 7
After the Storm

Before lessons the next evening, Lee and Bella told everyone about their adventure in old Gore's attic.

"What?" said Big Herb, between chomps of chocolate Screme Egg. "You mean old Gore has made Miss Fitt even worse? How can she be worse than she was yesterday? It took me so long to do my maths homework

I didn't get into my coffin till it was almost daylight."

"We don't know what happened to Boris," said Bella. "I hope he didn't have to spend the whole day hiding in the attic from old Gore and Miss Fitt!"

STOMP! STOMP! STOMP! STOMP!

"Yikes," said Lee. "Here she comes! Where's Billy?"

"He's late," said Bella. "Miss Fitt will go ballistic!"

As the stomping got closer,

Mr Gore suddenly appeared with his toolbag and pretended to check the classroom door, which was still broken from the night before. But he kept glancing at the class and chuckling unpleasantly.

"Look at him," whispered Lee. "He's waiting to see the results of the Monster Mega Charger."

STOMP! STOMP! STOMP! STOMP!

A few seconds later, Miss Fitt stood in the doorway.

"Good mornink, Miss Fitt!" smarmed Gore. "Anysink you need, Your Monstrosity, just let me know!"

Miss Fitt stomped to the front of the class. And just at that moment, Billy hurtled through the door.

The whole class gasped in horror. Poor Billy! What would Miss Fitt do?

Mr Gore smirked and rubbed
his hands together in glee.
Little flakes of finger snowed
down onto his boots.

"I-I'm really s-sorry I'm late,
Miss!" panted Billy in terror.
Miss Fitt stared at him.

"M-my watch stopped," said
Billy. "I-it got wet in the
rain."

The other
children held their
breaths. No one
dared to move.
Miss Fitt
opened her mouth.

And smiled.

"Never mind, Billy," she chuckled. "These things happen. Just run along and sit down, there's a dear."

The whole class gasped again – in disbelief.

"S-sorry, Miss?" said Billy, not quite daring to move.

"I do hope your watch can be mended," Miss Fitt went on. "Perhaps Mr Gore would be kind enough to look at it for you?"

Mr Gore had stopped rubbing his hands together.

His mouth had fallen open and he was making a strange gurgling sound.

"Dear me, are you all right, Mr Gore?" said Miss Fitt. "You look a little green."

"That's just his normal colour!" whispered Lee to Bella.

"I-I'm... fine," croaked Mr Gore. "But you... you're supposed to be... I thought..."

"Oh good," interrupted Miss Fitt firmly. "I'm delighted you're well. Now do be a dear and fix Billy's watch. By lunchtime?"

Billy handed over his watch. He still couldn't quite believe what was happening. Nor could anyone else.

Mr Gore glared at Billy and stuffed the watch into his overalls.

"Goodbye, Mr Gore!" said Miss Fitt brightly.

Old Gore shuffled out of the classroom, muttering very rude things about vampires.

Billy sat down next to Lee and Bella.

"Wow! What's happened to Miss Fitt?" he whispered.

"No idea," shrugged Lee. "Pretty cool though, isn't it?"

"Mmm," said Bella. "Let's see what she's like in maths first."

"Now then, class," said

Miss Fitt. "Today we shall start with... But what are you doing, my dears?"

"Getting out our maths books, Miss," said several glum voices at once.

"Maths?" said Miss Fitt. "Really?"

She checked the timetable.

"Good gracious!" she said. "Who on earth has been making you do so much maths? Dear me. This will never do!"

Miss Fitt grabbed a board

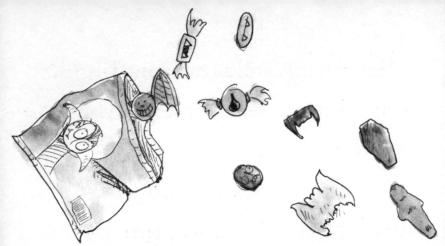

wiper and rubbed out all her
changes of the night before.
Then she crossed out all
the normal maths lessons
and wrote EXTRA BREAK
instead.

"I find maths so terribly
dull," said Miss Fitt. She took
a brown paper bag out of her
handbag. "Now, who would
like a sweet?"

At lunchtime the first thing Lee, Bella and Billy did was turn into bats and zoom up to the clock tower. They were relieved to find Boris safe and well.

"What happened last night?" said Lee. "Why didn't you follow us out of the attic?"

"Well," began Boris. "Remember when Miss Fitt woke up and said 'Vampires'?"

"Oh yeah," said Lee. "That was really freaky."

"Too right!" said Boris. "I

got such a fright I whacked my head on one of the knobs on the Monster Mega Charger. It was behind some wires and I hadn't noticed it before. When I looked closer I saw the knob was marked Horrometer."

"Hey!" said Billy. "That's the special knob I was looking for!"

"The Horrometer had ten settings," Boris went on. "From 1. Sweet and Nice to 10. Scary and Nasty. The knob was set to number 10, but I just had time to switch it to 1 before the lightning struck the conductor."

"Fantastic!" said Lee. "So Miss Fitt got a super-duper double-dose of NICENESS!"

"That's right," said Billy. "Old Gore must have changed her setting."

"Hang on," wondered Lee. "That still doesn't explain why you didn't leave the attic when we did."

"I got a bit tangled in the wires," said Boris. "By the time I freed myself old Gore was heading my way, so I hid behind the machine until he went to bed. Then I just flew back here."

Just above their heads, the school clock struck one.

"One o'clock! Yikes, we'd better get back and eat lunch," said Lee.

"Do you know what?" said Billy. "Miss Fitt gave us so many sweets I don't think

I can manage my raw steak sandwich."

"Oh, just give it to Big Herb," laughed Bella.

"Bye, Boris," called Lee as they fluttered out of the clock tower. "And thanks for saving us from two whole weeks of maths!"

The End

Hungry for more?
Get your teeth
into the next
Vampire School
adventure

Humorous chapter books, perfect for children beginning to read on their own, these young vampires' adventures will appeal to girls and boys alike.

Vampire School
Stage Fright

St.Orlok's is ready for its big phantomime -*Snow Fright and the Seven Dwarfs*. The mummy, werewolf, zombie and vampire parents are assembled. Bella is Snow Fright while Lee and Billy are two of the seven dwarfs - Gappy, Snappy, Flappy, Creepy, Chompy, Gnashful and Shock. But after an exhausting lesson of swooping, swerving and skulking, Bella isn't feeling very well. How will the show go on?

Vampire School
Casketball Capers

Lee, Billy and Bella are all on the St. Orlok's casketball team.

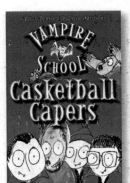

(That's the vampire version of basketball, in case you've never played it.) They're all getting ready for a big game against the Chaney Street werewolves. But when the other team arrives, it seems that some of them aren't planning on playing a fair game. Lee needs to come up with a plan – fast! Will he manage to foil the cheats before the final whistle?